LARGE PRINT 6 IN 1 EARLY READERS

AWESOME
FOLK TALES

SHREE BOOKS

Awesome Folk Tales
ISBN: 978-93-5049-406-6

First Edition: 2013

© Shree Book Centre

Printed in India

Retold by
Sunita Pant Bansal

Published by

SHREE BOOK CENTRE

8, Kakad Industrial Estate, S. Keer Marg
Off L.J. Road, Matunga (W)
Mumbai - 400016 (India)
Tel : 91-22-24377516 / 24374559
Telefax: 91-22-24309183
E-mail: sales@shreebookcentre.com

CONTENTS

PREFACE

Ever wondered why the sun rises so early in the morning or why cats love to sit in the kitchen? We often take these things for granted. But everything around us has a story of how it came into being.

Folk tales illustrate a lesson, moral value, belief or custom that is considered extremely important by a particular folk culture. Initially passed down orally from one generation to another, these timeless tales give us a taste of our culture and tradition that differs from state to state. Some of these tales will make your children think, laugh, wonder, and will also help them in discovering hidden wisdom.

This book, a carefully-picked bouquet of six moral-based stories, has colourful illustrations. The simple language makes reading easier for your children, and the dialogue blurbs allow the characters to speak their mind. The meanings of difficult words at the end of the book will help your children to build their vocabulary.

Why Cats Became Domesticated

The State of Gujarat has many interesting folk tales that are passed on from one generation to another. These folk tales have gained widespread popularity. One such tale is about how wild cats came to live among people.

Once there lived a lonely Cat in a forest. She did not have friends. So she decided that she would make some good and strong friends who would protect her during difficult times.

One day, the Cat met a Fox and asked him, "Dear Fox, I am lonely and have no friends. I would like to make the strongest animal in the forest my friend. It is good to have a strong friend. Could you please tell me who the strongest animal is?"

The Fox thought, 'Why should I name the other animals? I will make her believe that I am the strongest animal and then she will respect me.'

So, he said, "Dear Cat, I am the strongest animal in the forest and I will be your friend."

The Cat was very happy to hear that. The Cat and the Fox stayed together as good friends for many days.

One day, the Fox stole the Lion's food while he was away. When the Lion came to know about this, he killed the Fox out of anger. The Cat was very sad to lose her only friend. But she thought, 'The Lion is the strongest of all the animals. The Fox lied to me. So, I shall go to the Lion and be his friend.'

She offered a hand of friendship to the Lion, and he accepted. The Lion and the

Cat lived as good friends for many days.

One day, they went for a walk together and met an Elephant. The Lion and the Elephant had an argument about each other's strength. The Lion began to fight with the Elephant. The fight went on for a long time, and finally the Elephant killed the Lion.

The Cat was very sad to lose her friend. She thought, 'What shall I do? The Lion was nice to me. I have no friend now. But, it seems that the Elephant is stronger than the Lion. It will be convenient for me if the Elephant becomes my friend. I shall go to the Elephant and be his friend.'

She offered her friendship to the Elephant, and he accepted. They were friends for many days.

One day, they went for a walk and met a Hunter in the forest. The Hunter shot the Elephant with his gun and killed him for his tusks.

The Cat was sad to lose another friend,

but she thought, 'The Man is stronger than the Elephant.'

So she decided to be friends with the Man. She went to the Man and asked, "May I come with you to your home?"

"All right, come with me. Let us go home together," he said.

Soon, they reached the Man's home. His

wife met him at the door and took his gun from him.

The Cat was surprised and thought, 'Oh, the Woman is the strongest of all! She can take the hunter's gun from him, and he does not fight with her. He does not even say a word!'

The Man sat down at the dining table and

the Woman went to the kitchen to bring food for the Man. The Cat followed the Woman and went to the kitchen thinking, 'The Woman even gives food to the Man. So, she must be very strong and powerful. It will benefit me if I stay with her. Besides she will give me food too.' So the Cat decided to stay with the Woman forever.

That is why we always see a cat in the kitchen at a woman's feet. Thus, the cat stayed with humans and became a domesticated pet.

Moral: It is always wise to choose friends carefully.

A House In The Sky

Folk tales of Odisha are very famous for their moral values. One such story is that of a poor man who was known for his wit.

Once upon a time, there lived a poor man named Abhilas. He was quite popular for his intelligence. Abhilas had a policy

that he would never borrow money from anyone, even during crisis.

He often said, "Rich people take advantage of the poor by lending money and adding interest to it."

Abhilas often joked about the rich people's bad deeds. He did not even spare the Village Chief from his teasing. So, all the rich people in his village disliked him. They wanted to kill Abhilas, and always plotted against him to put him in trouble.

One day, the Chief called Abhilas and said, "I hear that you are very clever, Abhilas! Can you build me a house in the sky in three days? You may have as many men as you need. But remember, if you fail to

Can you build a house in the sky?

build a house in the sky, my soldiers will kill you!"

"I shall build it, my Chief," said Abhilas confidently and went home. He understood that the rich people had schemed to hurt him through this plan. So, he began to think of a plan to outwit the Chief and the rich people.

A bright idea struck Abhilas. He made a huge kite. Then he tied a bell and a long string to it. When the wind blew, the kite rose high up in the air. But it did not fly far because Abhilas had tied the string to a tree.

The next day, all the people of the town heard the bell ringing. They looked up and

saw a dark spot in the sky. The Chief saw the spot too.

Abhilas came up to the Chief and said, "Chief, your house in the sky will be ready soon. Do you hear the bell ringing? The workers are ringing the bell from the sky because they need some boards for the roof of the house. Please ask your soldiers to climb up to the sky with the boards."

"But how will my soldiers climb up to the sky?" asked the puzzled Chief.

"Oh, there is a way up. Please follow me," said Abhilas.

So the Chief ordered his soldiers to follow Abhilas with some boards. They came to the tree and saw the string there.

"This is the way to the sky," said Abhilas. "Climb up the string and you will soon reach the house that is being constructed in the sky."

The soldiers tried to climb up the string, but could not do that. They felt very foolish.

"Try again, try again! Our Chief will be

very angry if you don't carry the boards up to his house in the sky!" said Abhilas teasingly. Tired of trying to climb up the string, they gave up and returned home.

Then, the soldiers went to the Chief and said, "Chief! Please forgive us. No man can climb up to the sky, at least not with the help of a string!"

The Chief thought for a while and said, "That's right. Nobody can do that."

Abhilas was right behind him. He said to the Chief, "Chief, if you knew that, then why did you ask me to build a house in the sky?"

The ashamed Chief could not give any answer. Abhilas promptly went to the tree,

cut the string and took away the kite. He went home and had a good sleep.

The Chief felt embarrassed by his own foolishness. He scolded all the rich people for forcing him to join them in plotting against Abhilas. The rich people in that village never ever troubled Abhilas again.

Clever Abhilas taught the Chief and the rich people a good lesson about how to treat everyone with kindness and respect.

Moral: Treat everyone with respect and love.

The Greedy Jackal

Once upon a time, in the forests of Assam, there lived a Jackal.

One day, a thorn got stuck in the Jackal's paw. "Ouch!" he cried, as he walked along a path in the forest. "What shall I do? Who will help me?"

Then he met an Old Woman. "Dear Granny," he said, "Please pull the thorn out of my paw."

The kind Old Woman pulled it out. The Jackal thanked her and went away. Soon, he came back and asked, "Where is my thorn, Granny?"

"I don't know," answered the confused

Old Woman. "Who needs a thorn?"

Then the Jackal cried, "Oh, where is my thorn? I need it very much."

The Old Woman said, "Don't cry. Here is an egg for you."

The Jackal took the egg and ran away with it. He came to a village and knocked at the first door. A Man opened it.

The Jackal asked, "May I stay with you tonight? It is late and cold."

"Please come in," answered the Man.

The Jackal came in. "May I put my egg on this plate?" he asked.

"Yes, of course, you can," the Man replied.

In the night, the Jackal got up quietly, ate the egg and put the shell back on the plate.

In the morning, the Jackal asked, "Where is my egg?"

"I don't know," said the Man.

The Jackal began to cry, "Oh, my egg! Your cat ate it in the night!"

The Man gave him a hen instead of the egg.

The Jackal took the hen and ran away with it. He reached the next village in

the evening. There he knocked at the first door and asked the Woman who opened the door, "May I stay the night with you, please? It is so cold outside!"

"Please, come in," said the Woman.

"And where can I keep my hen?" asked the Jackal. "Let the hen stay with our goat," the Woman said.

In the night the Jackal got up quietly and ate the hen. In the morning he said, "Let us go and get my hen."

But there was no hen! There were only feathers and bones on the ground. The Jackal cried, "Oh, my beautiful grey hen! Your goat ate it in the night!"

The Woman apologised and gave him

one of the goat's kids instead of the hen. The Jackal thanked the Woman and ran away.

He came to another village. It was almost evening when he knocked at the first house. "May I stay the night in your house?" he asked the Man who opened the door. "I am very tired."

"Please come in," said the Man.

"Where may I put my little kid?" asked the Jackal. "Tie it to the end of my son's cot," said the Man.

At night, the Jackal ate up the kid and put its bones on the boy's cot.

In the morning, the Jackal asked, "Where is my little kid?"

They went to the boy's cot. But instead of the kid, there were only bones.

"Oh, my sweet little kid! Your son ate it in the night!" cried the Jackal.

The Man was shocked and said, "Don't cry. I shall give you a big goat instead of your little kid." "No, I don't want the goat! Give me your son!"

"All right, go out and wait at the door," said the Man.

Then the Man brought him a big bag and said, "Here is the boy. He is inside this bag."

The Jackal took the bag and went away quickly. He tried to run, but he couldn't. The bag was very heavy.

Here is the boy.

'Why is this boy so heavy?' thought the Jackal. 'Perhaps the Man has put stones into the bag!'

He opened the bag and two big dogs jumped out of it! In a minute they tore the Jackal to pieces.

Moral: One must not be greedy.

Clever Mahamood

Long ago, there lived a King in Uttar Pradesh. Writers, poets and musicians from many places came to see him. The King liked to hear their stories, poems and music.

But there was one man whom the King

liked the most. His name was Mahamood.
He knew many tricks, sang funny songs
and danced well. He could make the King
laugh and the people called Mahamood,
'The Fool of the King.'

There was one thing that the King did not
like about Mahamood. He ate all the time-
from morning till night. The King thought,

'My poor Mahamood will die soon if he continues to eat so much!'

Thus, the King called all his ministers and said, "Listen! For one day you must not give Mahamood anything to eat. Do not give him even a piece of bread! He must not even sit at my table."

So, the next day there was no place for

Mahamood at the King's table. He went close to the wall and stood there. He thought, 'I shall wait. Soon the servants will bring me food and drink.'

But the servants did not bring him anything.

Mahamood did not ask for food, because he was afraid of the King.

Poor Mahamood was very hungry. Then, one of the servants dropped a little piece of bread by mistake. Mahamood quickly picked it up thinking, 'Now I have something to eat. I shall eat it when the King is not looking at me.'

When dinner was over, the poets read their poems, the musicians played and the

What a performance!

I heard you have a donkey.

dancing girls began their beautiful dances. 'Now the King is watching the dancing girls,' thought Mahamood, 'I shall eat my piece of bread.' But the King was watching Mahamood all the time. He asked the musicians to stop, called Mahamood and asked, "I heard that you have a donkey. Where did you get it from?"

"I bought it from the market, Your Highness," answered Mahamood.

Again, the musicians started playing. Then Mahamood wanted to eat his piece of bread. But the King asked him to come near and asked, "How much did you pay for your donkey in the market?"

Mahamood put the bread in his pocket

quickly and answered, "Sixteen gold coins, Your Highness."

Whenever Mahamood tried to eat his piece of bread, the King asked him a question. Finally, Mahamood could not stand it any longer. He was very hungry and tired. When the feast was over, Mahamood ran to the kitchen, but it was locked and Mahamood had only his small piece of bread to eat. He ate it and went to his room. But he could not sleep. He was very hungry.

Then he ran to the King's room. He knocked on the door. The King asked angrily, "Who is knocking on my door so late?"

"Your Highness," said Mahamood. "I am sorry, but I must tell you that I did not buy

my donkey from the market, but from the next town."

The King told him to go away. A few minutes later, Mahamood knocked on the door again. "Your Highness, I told you a lie this afternoon. I did not pay sixteen gold coins for the donkey. I paid twenty gold coins for it."

"Oh, you fool!" cried the angry King. "I will cut off your head for your silly tales about the donkey and give your body to the jackals!"

Mahamood smiled, "Oh, yes, I know that. But before I die may I say my last wish?"

"What is your last wish?"asked the King.

"My last wish is to have a good supper."

The King laughed and asked his servants to bring the best food to his room. He sat down at the table with Mahamood. They ate and laughed till morning. Thereafter, Mahamood never had a day without food.

Moral: At times, humour and wit pay off.

The Small Red Bird

On the hills of Himachal Pradesh, there once lived a Man with his Wife. They were very poor and always hungry. The Man often went to the forest in search of small animals and birds. But he was a bad hunter, and sometimes brought home only a small bird.

One day, the Man went to the forest. But it was a very bad day for him. He did not find even a small bird.

He was tired and sad. He sat down under a tree to rest. Suddenly, he heard the sweet song of a bird. He looked up and saw a small Bird with red feathers.

The Bird said, "Dear Man, I see you every

day in this forest. I know that you are poor and hungry, so I want to help you. I will give you one of my feathers.

Take it home and cook it. You can come back tomorrow and I will give you another feather."

The Bird was a magical fairy in disguise. Its feathers had great powers. The

grateful Man thanked the Bird and went home with the feather.

His Wife was angry with him when she saw that he had brought nothing but a small red feather.

The Man put the feather into a pot of boiling water, and then told his Wife about the kind Bird.

"Silly, how can the feather become food? You must catch the Bird and kill it. Then we can cook the Bird and eat it," said his Wife.

The Man did not answer. But when his Wife looked into the pot, she saw a good dinner magically appearing in place of the feather.

That night the Man and his Wife had a sumptuous meal after a long time.

Then onwards, every day, the Man went to the forest and the small Bird gave him a red feather that made dinner for him and his Wife.

Thus, the Man and the Bird became good friends.

However, the Man's Wife was very greedy. Every day she would tell her husband, "We should not have one feather a day. We must have the whole Bird. Then we can cook two, three or four feathers every day, and we can have as much food as we like."

The Man was very angry at his Wife's

greediness. He told her, "The Bird is my friend. I will not kill it. Instead, we must thank it for helping us in our difficult times."

But the Wife was not satisfied with her husband's explanation.

She wanted to own the Bird so that she could take as many feathers as she wished.

She decided, 'Since my husband does not want to harm the Bird, I will go to the forest and bring it myself.'

Next day, the Wife followed her husband into the forest without his knowledge. Soon, the Wife heard the sweet song of the little red Bird. She even saw her husband talking to the Bird.

Blinded by greed, she took a stone and threw it at the Bird. The Bird fell down from the tree and died.

The Man shouted at his Wife for killing the innocent Bird who gave them food every day.

But the Wife said, "Now we will have plenty of food."

The Man was very sad for losing his best friend.

Then they went home with the dead bird. At home, the Wife pulled a small red feather off the Bird and put it into the hot water. She cooked it for a long time but the feather did not change into a meal.

It had lost its magical powers as the Bird was dead. The Man scolded his Wife for being greedy and selfish.

From that day on, they were always hungry.

Moral: One must always be thankful for what one has.

The Crocodile And The Hunters

The folk tales of Madhya Pradesh boast of many interesting stories. They have meaningful endings and teach valuable lessons.

A very long time ago, there was a big cave in a forest in Madhya Pradesh. The

top half of the cave was dry while the bottom was full of water. Many animals lived in the dry part, and an old Crocodile lived in the bottom part for years. He liked to lie in the water and sleep during summer. Sometimes, he came out of the cave for a short time during winter.

One day, a Hunter came to the forest with his bow and arrow. As he did not find any prey to hunt, he came near the cave to rest and eat his food. After he had his meal, he decided to get some water from the bottom of the cave. But he saw the Crocodile, who was sunbathing, and decided to kill him instead.

The Hunter aimed his bow and arrow at the Crocodile. Strangely, the Hunter became blind at once. Just as the Hunter dropped his arrow and rubbed his eyes, he began to see again!

Earlier, when the Crocodile noticed that the Hunter was trying to kill him, he could not get back into the water quickly because he was old. But when the Hunter was blinded for a minute, the old Crocodile was very happy that his life was saved! The Hunter saw the smiling Crocodile and aimed at him the second time. Again he became blind. The Crocodile was happy again!

The animals living on the dry part of the cave were hiding and watching the

Hunter. They too were glad that the Hunter was blinded when he tried to kill the Crocodile.

The shocked Hunter ran back to his village and told the people about the Crocodile. "As I aimed at him, I became blind. The minute the arrow fell out of my bow, I could see again," he said.

The people of the village did not believe him. They thought that the Hunter had lost his mind. The Hunter coaxed them to go with him to the cave and see the Crocodile for themselves.

A few men took their bows and arrows and headed towards the cave with the Hunter. They saw the old Crocodile lying in the

Here is the magical crocodile!

sun near the cave. To their amazement, when they aimed at him, they too became blind.

"Take your arrows from your bows," the Hunter cried. When they did so, they could see again! It was clear that the Crocodile had some magical powers!

'No man can kill me,' thought the happy

Crocodile and went back to the cave. The other animals in the cave were happy too. For, the magical Crocodile prevented the Hunters from entering the cave. They thanked the Crocodile for saving their life as well.

For a very long time, all the hunters stopped going to that forest to kill animals.

They feared the magical Crocodile. They knew that nobody could kill it with bows and arrows. In those days, Hunters knew nothing about guns.

A few years later, some young men with guns came to the forest to hunt.

One among them killed the Crocodile with his gun. He said to the others,

"Look, I managed to kill the Crocodile. He was not magical at all. It was the strong sunlight that blinded the eyes of the hunters, with a bow and arrow, for a few seconds. That's why they could see only after a while."

The other animals started becoming prey to hunters soon. They were very sorry to

Good meat! What do you say?

lose the Crocodile, as it had protected their lives. Sadly, the old Crocodile's magic worked only against bows and arrows. It did not work against guns.

Moral: It is important to protect our wildlife.

MEANINGS OF DIFFICULT WORDS

Why Cats Became Domesticated

Benefit : an advantage; help; aid

Domesticated : tamed or adapted to domestic use

Popularity : the state of being widely admired, accepted, or sought after

Widespread : common and occurring widely, or affecting many people or places

Lonely : without friends

Argument : a discussion involving different points of view

A House In The Sky

Outwit : to surpass in cleverness or cunning; outsmart

Plotted : to make a secret plan to do something wrong, harmful, or illegal

Promptly	:	with little or no delay; quickly
Schemed	:	a plan to do something illegal or dishonest
Crisis	:	a difficult condition
String	:	a rope or a cord
Embarrassed	:	feeling or caused to feel uneasy
Popular	:	commonly liked or approved
Policy	:	a plan of action
Construct	:	to build; to make or form by combining or arranging parts

The Greedy Jackal

Kid	:	a young goat
Paw	:	the foot of an animal
Confuse	:	to be unable to think with clarity or act with intelligence
Quietly	:	making little or no noise
Heavy	:	of great weight; difficult to lift or move

Clever Mahamood

Fool : one who acts unwisely on a given occasion

Silly : exhibiting lack of wisdom or good sense; foolish

Wit : the natural ability to perceive and understand; intelligence

Tired : loss of energy

The Small Red Bird

Sumptuous : rich and superior in quality; lavish

Greedy : excessively desirous of food or wealth

Grateful : appreciative of benefits received; thankful

Satisfied : content; happy

Magical : produced by magic

Suddenly : happening without warning; all of a sudden

Disguise	:	to hide the truth or actual character
Greedy	:	having or showing a selfish desire for something

The Crocodile And The Hunters

Coaxed	:	to persuade someone gently to do something or go somewhere
Prey	:	an animal hunted or caught for food
Sunbathing	:	exposing the body to the sun
Valuable	:	of great importance, use, or service
Meaningful	:	having meaning, function or purpose
Prevent	:	to keep from happening
Boast	:	to possess or own; a cause for pride
Valuable	:	a thing that is of great worth